For Ellen!

BEACH LANE BOOKS
An imprint of Simon & Schuster Children's Publishing Division
1230 Avenue of the Americas, New York, New York 10020
© 2023 by Jan Thomas
Book design © 2023 by Simon & Schuster, Inc.
For information about special discounts for bulk purchases, please contact Simon & Schuster
Special Sales at 1-866-506-1949 or business@simonandschuster.com.
The Simon & Schuster Speakers Bureau can bring authors to your live event. For more
information or to book an event, contact the Simon & Schuster Speakers Bureau at
1-866-248-3049 or visit our website at www.simonspeakers.com.
The text for this book was set in Chaloops Galaxy.
The illustrations for this book were rendered digitally.
Manufactured in China
0423 SCP
First Edition
10 9 8 7 6 5 4 3 2 1
CIP data for this book is available from the Library of Congress.
ISBN 9781665939997
ISBN 9781665940009 (ebook)

PROBLEM SOLVED!

Jan Thomas

Beach Lane Books • New York   London   Toronto   Sydney   New Delhi

PROBLEM SOLVED!!!